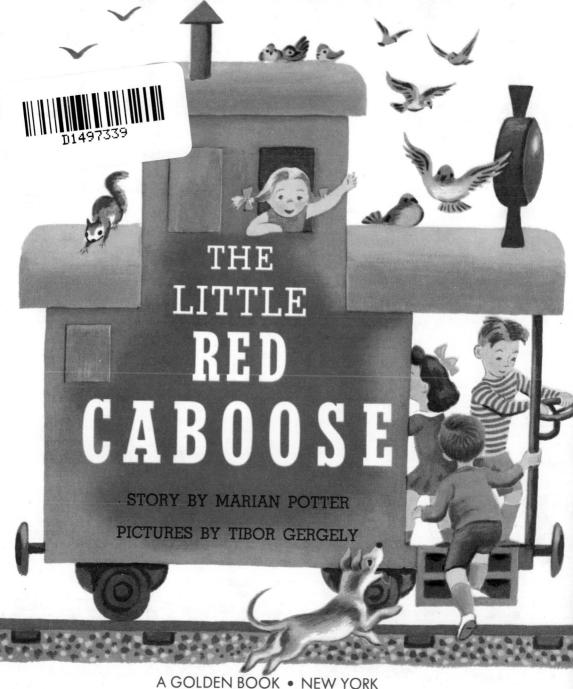

THE
LITTLE
RED
CABOOSE

STORY BY MARIAN POTTER

PICTURES BY TIBOR GERGELY

A GOLDEN BOOK • NEW YORK
Western Publishing Company, Inc.
Racine, Wisconsin 53404

FOR ANDREW, PAMELA, AND REBECCA

The little red caboose
always came last.

First came the big black engine,
puffing and chuffing.

Then came the boxcars,

then the oil cars,

then the coal cars,

then the flat cars.
Sometimes they were
switched around in different ways.

But the little red caboose
always came last.

Boys and girls waved
at the big black engine.

They listened to the boxcars
and the oil cars
and the coal cars
and the flat cars
go *clickety clack.*

But by the time the little red caboose
came along, the boys and girls
were turning away.
Because the little red caboose
always came last.

"Oh, smoke!" said the little red caboose.
"I wish I were a flat car
or a coal car or an oil car
or a boxcar, so boys and
girls would wave at me.

"How I wish I were a big black engine,
puffing and chuffing way up
at the front of the train!

"But I'm just the little old red caboose.
Nobody cares for me."

One day the train
started up a mountain.
Up went the big black engine.
Up went the boxcars.
Up went the oil cars.

Up went the coal cars.
Up went the flat cars.
Up went the little red caboose.

"Hang on tight, little caboose,"
called the flat car.
"This is a long tall mountain.
And you are the last car
on the train."
    "Don't I know it!"
sighed the little red caboose.
"Poor me!"

The train went slower
and slower and s-l-o-w-e-r.
Soon it was hardly moving.
It looked as if that train
could not get up the mountain.

"Look out, little caboose!"
called the flat car.
"The train is starting to slip
back down this long tall mountain!"
   "Not if I can help it!"
said the little red caboose.

And he slammed on his brakes.
And he held tight to the tracks.
And he kept that train
from sliding down the mountain!

Then, *bump!*
The little red caboose
felt something push him
from behind.

It was two big black engines.
They pushed the train up to the top
of the mountain.

"We couldn't have done it,"
said the big black engines,
"if it had not been for the
little red caboose."
    Everyone cheered.
And the little red caboose
nearly burst with pride.

Now, children wave at the big black engine and at all the cars.

But they save their biggest waves for the little red caboose. Because the little red caboose saved the train.